This book is dedicated to children

who are lost and alone, and to those

who help them.

CANDLEWICK PRESS

The Day War Came

Nicola Davies

illustrated by Rebecca Cobb

THE DAY WAR CAME there were flowers on the windowsill and my father sang my baby brother back to sleep.

My mother made my breakfast, kissed my nose, and walked with me to school.

That morning I learned about volcanoes.

I sang a song about how tadpoles

turn at last into frogs.

I drew a picture of a bird.

Then, just after lunch, war came.

At first, just like a spattering of hail,

a voice of thunder . . .

then all smoke and fire and noise that I didn't understand.

It came across the playground.

It came into my teacher's face.

It brought the roof down

and turned my town to rubble.

I can't say the words that tell you
about the blackened hole
that had been my home.

All I can say is this:

War took everything.

War took everyone.

I was ragged, bloody, all alone.

I ran. Walked over fields and roads and mountains
in the cold and mud and rain;

rode on the back of trucks, in buses;

went on a boat that leaked and almost sank;

then up a beach where shoes lay empty in the sand.

I ran until I couldn't run,

until I reached a row of huts

and found a corner with a dirty blanket

and a door that rattled in the wind.

But war had followed me.

It was underneath my skin,

behind my eyes,

and in my dreams.

It had taken possession of my heart.

I walked and walked to try to drive war out of myself,

to try to find a place it hadn't reached.

But war was in the way that doors shut when I came down the street.

It was in the way that people didn't smile, and turned away.

I came to a school.

I looked in through the window.

They were learning all about volcanoes,

and singing, and drawing birds.

I went inside.

My footsteps echoed in the hall.

I pushed the door, and faces turned

toward me but the teacher didn't smile.

She said, "There is no room for you,

you see. There is no chair for you to sit on.

You have to go away."

And then I understood that

war had gotten here, too.

I turned around and went back to the hut, the corner,
and the blanket, and crawled inside.

It seemed that war had taken all the world
and all the people in it.

The door banged. I thought it was the wind—but a child's voice spoke.

"I brought you this," he said, "so you can come to school."

It was a chair.

A chair for me to sit on and learn about volcanoes, and sing, and draw birds.

And drive the war out of my heart.

He smiled and said, "My friends have brought theirs, too,

so all the children here can come to school."

Out of every hut a child came,
and we walked together
on a road lined with chairs.

Pushing

back the war

with every step.

Of the world's 22.5 million refugees—people who have fled their countries because of war or suffering—more than half are children. And too often countries with the resources to help these displaced people turn them away instead. Recently, the United States limited the annual number of refugees it will accept to just 50,000. In the spring of 2016, the government of the UK refused to give sanctuary to 3,000 unaccompanied child refugees. At about the same time, I heard a story about a refugee child being refused entry to a school because there wasn't a chair for her to sit on. Out of that, this poem was written. It was first published on the *Guardian* newspaper's website alongside images of an empty chair by illustrators Jackie Morris and Petr Horáček. In the days that followed, hundreds and hundreds of people posted images of empty chairs, with the hashtag #3000chairs, as symbols of solidarity with those children who had lost everything and had nowhere to go—and no chance of an education. I want this story to remind us all of the power of kindness and its ability to give hope for a better future.

—*Nicola Davies*

Founded by a group of friends who saw the worsening situation for refugees in Europe and wanted to do something about it, Help Refugees now supports more than seventy projects to aid refugees worldwide with funding, food, shelter, and volunteers. Filling gaps left by governments and large NGOs, Help Refugees responds to the genuine needs of refugees and displaced populations in a fast, flexible, and empowering way. #Chooselove

Go to www.helprefugees.org to learn more about its work and how you can help.

First US paperback edition 2020

Library of Congress Catalog Card Number 2018956977
ISBN 978-1-5362-0173-4 (hardcover)
ISBN 978-1-5362-1593-9 (paperback)

20 21 22 23 24 25 CCP 10 9 8 7 6 5 4 3 2 1

Printed in Shenzhen, Guangdong, China

This book was typeset in Filosofia OT.
The illustrations were done in pencil, colored pencil, and watercolor.

Candlewick Press
99 Dover Street
Somerville, Massachusetts 02144

www.candlewick.com